Attention, *HOP* fans!
Look for these items
when you read this book.
Can you find them all?

Bongos

**The Egg of
Destiny**

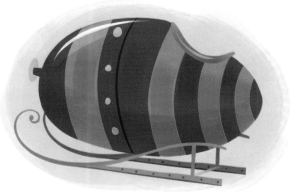

Sleigh

Marshmallows

First edition: February 2011

ISBN 978-0-316-12901-5

10 9 8 7 6 5 4 3 2 1

CW

Printed in the United States of America

Meet the Easter Bunny

Based on the film *HOP*
Story by Cinco Paul & Ken Daurio
Screenplay by Cinco Paul & Ken Daurio and Brian Lynch
Adapted by Lucy Rosen
Pictures by Pete Oswald

LITTLE, BROWN & COMPANY
LB kids

E.B. is a very special rabbit.
He can talk and play the drums.
Plus, his dad is the Easter Bunny!

E.B. and his dad
live on Easter Island.
That is where Easter candy is made.

"Would you like to see
where your father works?"
asks E.B.'s dad.
"Oh boy, would I!" says E.B

E.B. grabs his bongo drums
and follows his dad
into a secret elevator.
They go underground to the Easter factory.

"Take a good look, son," says E.B.'s dad. "Someday this will all be yours."

E.B. cannot believe his eyes.
There is candy everywhere
of every shape and size!

Candied almonds, malted eggs, and jelly beans of all colors glide through the factory on moving belts.

"Let me show you how we do things around here," says E.B.'s dad.

12

"First things first.
The Easter Bunny makes sure
the candy gets made with care!"

E.B. looks around.
He sees bunnies painting eggs
and a group of chicks
carving a chocolate bunny.

E.B. is so happy
that he plays a little song
on his bongos.

The bunnies and chicks
dance while they work!

"It is up to the Easter Bunny
to make sure everything tastes great.
What is your favorite
Easter treat, son?" asks E.B.'s dad.

E.B. starts to answer.

"Oh, I like—"

"Wrong," his dad interrupts.

"Every candy is the Easter Bunny's favorite!"

"Follow me, son," says E.B.'s dad.
"There is someone I want you to meet."
E.B. walks behind his dad.

WHOOSH!
A chick on roller skates zooms by.
E.B. ducks behind a lollipop tree
to get out of the way!

19

"E.B., this is Carlos,"
says E.B.'s dad.
"Carlos is my right-hand chick
around here."

"It is nice to meet you," E.B. says
as he pops a marshmallow
into his mouth.

"What did you think
of the marshmallow?"
asks E.B.'s dad.

"Too much marsh,
not enough mallow?"
E.B. says as a guess.

"Very good!" says his dad.
"Carlos! Too much marsh!
Not enough mallow!"

"Too much marsh!
Not enough mallow!"
Carlos cries to the workers.

TOO MUCH MARSH!
NOT ENOUGH MALLOW!

"Once the candy is ready,
the Easter Bunny's next job
is to deliver it," says E.B.'s dad.
"We do that in the egg sleigh!"

24

"Doesn't Santa have a sleigh
just like it?" E.B. asks.
"We had one first!"
E.B.'s dad insists.

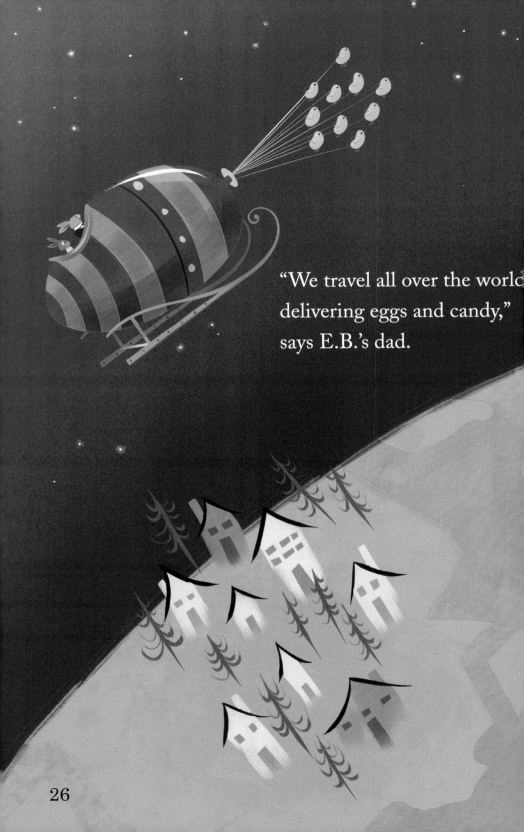

"We travel all over the world delivering eggs and candy," says E.B.'s dad.

"And just like that, it is Easter! The Easter Bunny's job is done."

"This is the last thing
I want to show you today,"
says E.B.'s dad.
"The Egg of Destiny!"

"One day, I will pass on
the Egg of Destiny to you.
Then you will be the Easter Bunny!"

E.B. is unsure.
Being the Easter Bunny
is a very big job.
He is not sure he can do it.
Without thinking,
E.B. starts to play the drums again.
Everyone in the factory starts to dance!

"Okay, Dad." E.B. smiles.
"I'll be the Easter Bunny,
as long as I can do it my way—
with a little rock and roll!"

E.B.'s dad gives him a big hug.
"You got it, son!"